The Sheep of
Poshington Hall Farm

The Trolls' Knees-Up
and
Ghostly Goings-On

Marcia Mason

Copyright © 2019 Marcia Mason

ISBN: 978-0-244-20762-5

PublishNation
www.publishnation.co.uk

A bit about the Author Marcia Mason

The Sheep of Poshington Hall Farm stories have been in my head for at least 50 years but I have been so busy in my life that it is only now since my wonderful husband Jim passed away and I retired that I've been able to fulfil my lifelong ambition to finish writing them and share them with you. I hope adults will enjoy reading them to children, and children will love listening and reading them too for many years to come and, maybe one day you will get the opportunity to visit the beautiful Lake District in England, Madeira, or Iceland.

Introduction to *The Sheep of Poshington Hall Farm*

Hekla and Freya live at Poshington Hall Farm in the Lake District. They look like many sheep with silly smiles, beautiful woollen fleeces and horns, but they are not. They are in fact Icelandic sheep that possess secret troll given magical powers in their fleeces and go on wonderful adventures. In this book the sheep join forces with the spectral army of Mungrisdale, their friendly Icelandic Lilts troll and the ghosts of Poshington Hall, to stop partying greedy flesh-eating trolls, helping themselves to the sheep and residents of the Farm and Hall.

The Sheep of Poshington Hall Farm Series

The Sheep of Poshington Hall Farm - Book 1

*The Sheep of Poshington Hall Farm's
Flying Visit to Iceland - Book 2*

*The Sheep of Poshington Hall Farm
Go on a Cruise - Book 3*

*The Sheep of Poshington Hall Farm
The Trolls' Knees-Up and Ghostly Goings-On - Book 4*

The Sheep of Poshington Hall Farm
books are dedicated to
my wonderful late husband Jim.

Chapter 1

The Troll Party Invitation

High on a tall old dusty twisted red brick Tudor chimney pot stack, atop the roof of Poshington Hall, sat the all-seeing wise old Wink-a-Puss owl. He began his waking up ritual. First, he exercised his gorgeous large shiny yellow eyes with their big black pupils, each blinked once, one at a time, then both together. He turned his head almost full circle for a good view and ruffled his feathers. Next he stretched his talons and exercised his wings, flexing them, of course, one at a time.

The silver moon was rising, so that meant it was time to get up.

Already his friend Barry the bat BHOM (Bat Hit Or Miss) postman had started his night delivery shift.

"Good evening Barry," hooted Wink-a-Puss. Barry whistled back a high-pitched greeting,

"Evening Mr Wink-a-Puss. Be warned, be warned."

Wink-a-Puss was alarmed; a bat warning from Barry meant big trouble ahead.

Mr Wink-a-Puss pressed Barry for more information, and so Barry told him that the following night was the December Winter Solstice, the darkest, shortest day and longest night that started with sunset in Iceland at 3.30pm, and finished the following day at 11.30am with just 5 hours of daylight, which gave the trolls plenty of time to celebrate their 'Knees-Up' over Poshington Hall Farm.

"You mean those trolls from the icy Nordic world?" enquired Wink-a-Puss in a concerned low hoot.

"That's right," Barry confirmed.

Wink-a-Puss knew all about the legendary troll get-togethers, but this one was a very big occasion in more ways than one. His Great Great Great Grandfather had told him all about it when he was a baby owlet. It was the one night that trolls who had been turned to stone by sunlight would re-awaken and join the ones that had avoided such a fate.

"But, why? Why Poshington Hall?" Wink-a-Puss puzzled.

Barry explained, "Apparently, it was because in his saga one night, after getting exceedingly drunk on a whole flagon of Moss schnapps with the other living trolls, the Icelandic Lilts troll had mentioned Hekla and Freya, the Icelandic sheep that lived at Poshington Hall Farm on the fells in the beautiful Lake District of England.

"He boasted about how he had once rescued lambs from being eaten in Iceland and how Hekla and Freya, the Icelandic sheep, came flying to collect them from him. To enable them to fly safety back to Poshington Hall, he had used magic to miniaturise them, and then had tucked them into Freya and Hekla's horns."

So it was, the curious trolls asked the Great Troll if they could have their 'Knees-Up' in the clouds above Poshington Hall, and he acceded to their request.

Barry showed Wink-a-Puss one of the invitations he had in his sack.

The invitation was hand-written on edible paper made from seaweed algae pressed in leaves, with goblin-gold lettering. The invitation requested attendees to bring food for the buffet, a dish, bowl, spoon, and a flagon or two of drink with them.

To eat, trolls use their fingers and spoons, never knives and forks. They tear flesh from bone with their sharp pointy teeth, then throw the bones and carcasses on the floor and these often land in the sea.

Chapter 2

Wink-a-Puss Makes a Decision

Wink-a-Puss knew most trolls were large lumps of misery, pretty solitary, sorrowful, unloved creatures, and consequently their main comfort in life was eating and drinking, which made them enormously fat. Most were nice once you got to know them, like the Lilts troll. However, some had developed nasty greedy streaks with a tendency to become grumpy.

Having slept for hundreds of years, most guests would have grown stiff from lack of exercise; they'd be even bigger than before they'd turned to stone in sunlight, with clumps of moss on their bellies, noses and ears. They would be pock-marked with old sea-bird nests. In fact, the lummoxes would be very ugly and badly behaved indeed, very hungry and extremely thirsty.

Troll drinking sessions were legendary, and after a couple of flagons they'd squabble a lot, fight, and wrestle. When arguments got very heated, some bit huge chunks out of others, which often resulted in the loss of noses, ears and fingers. They made terrible burping and farting noises and thought it was funny making a mess by throwing food and drink about, so long as they didn't have to clear it up. When trolls laugh it is raucous, very loud, and mostly insincere. Sometimes they emit deep growls mixed with insults.

Although the reunion was known as a 'Knees-Up', it was an absurd description since most attendees were so massive that it was doubtful that many could actually touch their toes, let alone get their knees up!

For entertainment, the Norse god Thor normally provided party crackers with thunderbolts in them for such occasions, but it was not unknown for Pegasus the winged horse to turn up, too, carrying thunderbolts in his saddle bags, sent as a gift from the Greek God Zeus.

"Very worrying, very worrying, with all those pregnant ewes," hooted Wink-a-Puss. He knew how much the trolls loved eating livestock, and worried about the safety of the Icelandic sheep and their unborn lambs in the barns, as well as the hardy Herdwick sheep, too, that lived all year round out on the fells. Most worrying of all was that some trolls had been known to eat humans!

He thanked Barry for the tip-off and bid him a safe shift.

So, the old Wink-a-Puss fluffed up his feathers again, looked all around, then up to the sky for inspiration as he needed to give the impending grave situation some very careful consideration and use his wisdom wisely.

After careful deliberation, he decided that there was only one thing for it, and that was a call to arms by waking up the ghosts of Poshington Hall, to join forces with the spectral army of Mungrisdale.

Being hidden folk like the trolls, they couldn't be killed, but they could protect the sheep and human flock. They would know the best way to deal with any menacing trolls.

Chapter 3

The Spectral Army of Mungrisdale
Are Summoned

Wink-a-Puss knew that the old Lord Poshington was a good friend of the commander of the Mungrisdale Spectral Army. So, softly, Wink-a-Puss hooted a special call to Lord Poshington's ghost, and in next to no time, Lord Poshington had flown from his family vault in the nearby church's crypt, which was housed under the altar, and joined Wink-a-Puss on the roof.

The wise old owl explained the situation to Lord Poshington who had no hesitation in offering his services. He told Wink-a-Puss that he'd go straightaway and have a word with his old chum, the Spectral Army commander Captain Archibald Cunningham.

Captain Cunningham was in charge of a band of ghost soldiers with consciences, who had been killed in various battles over the centuries, after killing others or being nasty and cowardly by putting others in danger. Their punishment prescribed by the gods was for them to put right their wrongs or march for all eternity. Once forgiven, they could rest a while or go on to new lives. Some even earned a place with the heroes in Valhalla (the hall of Nordic heroes, a kind of heaven ruled by the Norse god Thor).

Captain Archibald Cunningham joined the Army shortly after his army was defeated by the Jacobites at the Battle of Falkirk Muir. When he died in 1745, he was very unhappy, not only because of the defeat, but because he had fled the disaster using supply horses, leaving his men without supplies.

In his wanderings, Captain Cunningham had recruited many 'lost' soldiers from over the centuries including: Vikings, Saxons, Roundheads, Cavaliers, and Romans. Amongst the Romans was Septimius Severus Constantius, the only Roman Emperor to have died in England. He had been responsible for shoring up some of Hadrians wall, but had been taken ill attacking the Scots. When he died, he was very upset about not completing his mission to seize Scotland for the Roman Empire. As a member of the Mungrisdale Army he no longer had commanding power, but was happy to take his orders from Captain Cunningham. You see, in the spirit world there is no such thing as time. The only differences between the soldiers' shadows was their weaponry and uniform. But, regardless of time, they were always brothers-in-arms.

To prove that they still existed, the Army often showed up on Midsummer's Day to the living with psychic sensitivity at Mungrisdale in the Lake District of England. Their counterparts in France had appeared at Mons during the First World War and helped the outnumbered British troops in battle against the Germans.

Chapter 5

The Storm Begins

The next night, unaware of the impending reunion, the Icelandic sheep at Poshington Hall Farm we're settling down nicely for the night in their warm barn, while small mice and voles scurried about their business on the look out for food scraps, dodging cats and owls, who were also making their own plans for a Friday night take-away.

"Poo, yuk I can smell rotting cabbages tonight," said Beryl the farmer's wife.

"Me too, and ammonia. The sky is darkening, I can feel a storm brewing," said Farmer Joe.

Then a large crackle of lightning ripped through the sky followed swiftly by a loud rumble of thunder. The sheep in the barn started to become restless, and Bouncer the sheep dog barked loudly. Hekla and Freya knew from their fleeces something wasn't quite right. So, Farmer Joe put his mackintosh and rubber wellington boots on, pulled up his hood and, accompanied by Bouncer, went to check on the sheep. He unhooked his guitar from the barn wall and they both sat on a messy hay bale next to Mr Boohoo the scarecrow, and Joe began playing old folk ballads and sang softly to the sheep. The sheep loved listening to him, and despite the noise of the thunderstorm were soon sleeping soundly; all except for Hekla and Freya. Then, Farmer Joe went back to the house to finish his supper of mushroom and cheese omelette with crispy hand-cut chips. However, for safe-keeping, he asked Bouncer to remain in the barn to watch over the sheep for the night and to let him know immediately if anything was amiss.

"Who knows where that nasty smell on the wind is coming from. It's getting stronger," said Beryl, and then she remembered that the last time she had smelt something so bad had been in Iceland trying out the traditional fermented shark food Kæstur hákarl.

The sky was now very very dark and crowded with thundery clouds. A large drop of rain splashed on Wink-a-Puss's beak and he hooted loudly, "Find shelter, quick!" Then he flew from his chimney pot roost straight to the barn with the sheep and kept a look out for mice for his dinner.

Barry the bat and his family hid in their bat box that had been put up on a nearby wall by the local Wildlife Trust. It was a cosy safe spot for him, Mrs Bat, and their pups.

Chapter 6

The Troll Party Guests Arrive

Slowly the trolls began to arrive for their 'do' and roared greetings at each other like, "I haven't seen you for years!" It really was true for those who had been turned to stone by sunlight. Some were more jocular in their greeting by saying such things as, "How's your belly off for spots?" and "My, haven't you grown." Guests from Iceland included trolls from Hvitserkur, Vik, and

Dvergasteinn. Of course, the great trolls of the North; South, East and West were there, too. It was a huge occasion. Most brought massive flagons of mead, Moss schnapps, and Brennivín, a liquorish tasting Icelandic spirit, along with Icelandic pure water from the falls and Scandinavian fjords.

For food, they arrived with huge bulky sacks of slain cattle and sheep, which they duly emptied with a thump in heaped-up piles on the cloud tables. The Lilts troll's sack of food was small in comparison to the others, but smelt the worst of fermented shark and rotting cabbage.

Soon the hungry trolls were tucking into their food and guarding their own supplies from other sneaky guests. They swigged directly from their flagons or poured their drinks straight down each other's gurgling throats. The noise was deafening as they told each other about dreams they'd had and battles in dreamland. Sagas of the hot fires of Valhalla were always popular and included tales of heroic warrior encounters.

"More food, more food!" bellowed the trolls in between trying to out-sing each other with rude drinking songs, belching, and farting loudly as they ate.

Tubs of pepper, salt, and thick yellow mustard were laid out on the cloud table for seasoning. But, of course, the pepper soon filled the air as it was flung about, and the trolls that still had noses intact began sneezing loudly and shooting large snots like glue-guns from their flared nostrils. They had never learnt to use handkerchiefs. They roared with laughter as they stuck things to the tables and each other.

Then one of the trolls who had slept for more years than most and who had missed the previous 'Knees-Up' began joining the other trolls aggressively demanding more food. His large hairy, weedy belly rumbled and vibrated loudly. He had an even greater insatiable appetite than the others, and to make matters worse, suffered from worms. He started banging his spoon loudly on the echoing cloud table and shouting repeatedly for more food.

The rain lashed down and the thunder rolled, there was sheet lightning and bolts in the sky as the trolls danced and fought each other with magic spells.

The noise of the partying trolls was almost unbearable. Then the Great Troll of the West, who was the biggest meat eater of all with the largest pointy yellow teeth tinged with blood, finished his meat supply and in a terrifying voice commanded, "Let's fill our bellies with lambs and sheep."

All the trolls banged their fists on the table and began chanting, "Get the lambs." After a while, they started a new more terrifying chant, "Get the lambs and humans." The only silent voice was that of the Lilts troll, who decided to try and reason with the others. "Shouldn't you be eating vegetables to save the Earth from global warming?" he began.

"Why should we?" they argued.

"Well, because cattle and sheep fart (although he knew sheep weren't as bad) so much that they produce too much methane gas and that warms the planet, which melts the ice."

"But, we're hungry," said the other trolls.

The Lilts troll felt very guilty that he had brought the trolls to Poshington Hall. He now had to save the sheep and people, too.

Chapter 7

The Defence of Poshington
Hall Farm Begins

As food stocks dwindled, the trolls began squabbling and fighting even more over each other's food. The Great Troll of the North had had enough and banged his fist loudly on the table and bellowed, "Stop your fighting!" The Great Troll of the East coughed politely and told everyone to mend their ways. Then the Great Troll of the South let out a loud noisy burp for attention and he told the naughty trolls to pull themselves together.

At that command, the trolls began picking up ears and bits of noses and fingers, reuniting them with their owners using magical powers. Some, however, got the wrong parts! It took ages to swap parts over. Some trolls preferred their ncw noses.

Only the Great Troll of the West continued his worrying chant. He cared nothing for global warming. The trolls began getting drunk again, and soon started chanting with the Great Troll of the West.

Mr Wink-a-Puss had heard all the goings-on and began to ruffle his feathers and nervously click his beak. He knew things were desperate and it was time to act and rally the ghosts to help save the sheep, Farmer Joe, Jenny, and Beryl, as well as the living Poshington family, from being eaten by the hungry trolls.

After all, he thought it would only take just one swipe of a troll's hand from the clouds to easily scoop them all up from the barn, hall, and farmhouse.

Wink-a-Puss got really drenched in the pouring rain as with heavy wings he flew up to the tower of Poshington Hall and screeched to the ghosts, "Awake, awake! Rise up, ghosts, save your ancestral home and lands!" Lord Poshington was already on his way back, having rendezvoused with Captain Cunningham and the Spectral

Army. Slowly, the Poshington ancestors stirred from their graves and began to organise themselves in groups around the buildings. The living Poshington family, as always, were sleeping, oblivious to what was going on and the danger they, too, faced.

Suddenly a trumpet sounded, it could be heard above the thunderous storm. Wink-a-Puss looked to the horizon, from where the trumpeting was coming from, and saw Lord Poshington riding side-by-side on horseback with Captain Cunningham at the head of the Spectral Army.

The Commander of the Spectral Army was dressed in a magnificent plumed velvet tricorn hat. His soldiers were in their finest battledress. The Roman contingent wore polished helmets and breast plates over their fine woollen tunics and carried spears - some carried round shields known as scutums, whilst others used long shields and wide swords. Some of the foot soldiers carried staffs and spears. Of course, those who had served under the 'Butcher' The Duke of Cumberland at the battle of Culloden had canons and guns; they wore red jackets and black tricorn hats. Knights of old wore clanking suits of armour and metal helmets and carried lances and swords astride their faithful chargers. And all of the army were marching at a pace down the fell to Poshington Hall Farm to join the Poshington ghosts that surrounded the sheep barn, hall, and the farmhouse.

Then, since the Trolls still wouldn't listen to his pleadings not to eat the sheep, the Lilts troll jumped down from the sky and joined the spectral army as a hidden folk person to shield the sheep and humans from the meat eating trolls.

Bouncer the sheep dog began to bark loudly then started to whimper, so Farmer Joe pulled back the curtains to see what was going on, and to his amazement saw the band of ghosts. He rubbed his eyes in disbelief. Beryl, too, saw them, but they decided to stay put. Well wouldn't you?

The trolls shielded their eyes and reached down from the cloud to scoop up their food, but found their hands full of spears, lances and bites.

"Ouch!" they cried, and two of the biggest ugliest, hungriest monstrous trolls stepped down from the sky.

Although, the Lilts troll tried his level best to reason with the trolls, they wouldn't listen, so he threw bolts of lighting at them which he had got from Pegasus the winged horse's saddle bag. Still, the big trolls were unperturbed. Even though the Lilts troll had caused a few dents and the loss of a few chunks from the aggressive trolls' arms, fingers and legs, the meat-eating trolls continued their advance. The Lilts troll shouted desperately at the trolls, "Go back home, you greedy lot, and leave the sheep and human-folk alone!" But, still they kept coming for the sheep in the barn - they were determined to fill their bellies.

Chapter 8

Hekla and Freya's Magic
Saves the Flock

Hekla and Freya had already used their fleece magic to make themselves invisible, but the trolls could still see them.

The trolls growled loudly and raged as they got nearer and nearer to the sheep barn. The sheep had to think quickly on their hooves about what to do, and how they could help.

Hekla suddenly came up with a plan. "Let's use our magic to make ourselves bigger and fiercer than the trolls and send them packing back home."

Freya loved the idea and they licked their fleeces and said the magic words: "Galdur, Galdur make us bigger than the trolls, higher than the sky, make our fleeces spikier than the spikiest spike with curly wire springs to bounce the trolls back. Make our horns strong and activated with electricity like an electric fence. Make our eyes blink out thunderbolts and glow in the dark, O great troll."

Suddenly, the sheep began to shake. "Wow, I do feel odd, very very odd," said Hekla.

"Me too," Freya bleated.

In a swift moment the roof of the barn became a sheep hat as it lifted, high into the sky. The flock gasped in wonder. Bouncer barked loudly and ordered the flock to remain calm and to stand out of the way.

Mr Boohoo wasn't keen on getting wet as he was really a fair-weather scarecrow, and he made a huffing noise.

Farmer Joe, Jenny, Bouncer and Beryl looked on in astonishment. Time seemed to stand still.

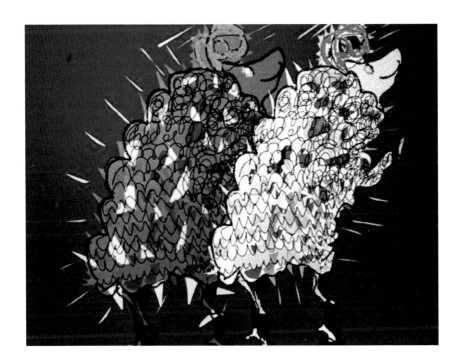

The sheep by now looked really ferocious and began bashing and bumping the trolls with their bodies and their fleeces glowed brightly as did their eyes that flashed thunderbolts at the menacing trolls.

Many of the remaining trolls in the sky became petrified before the night was out and were glad to be turned back to stone, and soon settled back to sleep once more in their Nordic lands. Those still in the sky that were never stoned in the first place, whooshed back home as quickly as they could. Still the sheep remained and stood their ground.

The army continued to rattle their sabres noisily and scream as they ran at the remaining trolls on the ground in such a terrifying manner that the trolls quickly retreated to the sky. Soon, not a single aggressive troll remained as they followed the other trolls back home to their Nordic regions.

The saga of the sheep became legendary.

The Lilts troll had put up a tremendous fight and lay exhausted and tearful on the ground with bits missing.

"Good work," said the ghost of Lord Poshington to the others and shook hands with the Spectral Army commander and what was left of the Lilts troll's right hand.

The sheep re-sized to 'normal' and removed their terrifying look - their fleeces were soft once more.

Then Hekla and Freya noticed that their friend the Lilts troll was hurt. "Don't worry Lilts, we'll help you and soon have you on the mend," said Hekla.

The Lilts troll briefly opened his eyes and tears of pain and sadness rolled down his cheeks. "Thank goodness you are alright," he whispered, then managed to smile at them before closing his eyes. There was no time to lose if they were to save him before dawn. Quickly, Hekla and Freya licked their coats, and then licked his wounds and said, "Galdur, Galdur make the Lilts troll strong and whole again." There was a last clap of thunder and a flash of lightning in the sky. The Lilts troll opened his eyes again. It was still dark, he stood up and he was his old self.

"Thank you, thank you so much Freya and Hekla for saving me again." The sheep were relieved that their magic had cured their friend Lilts. "I must be going now, before light, but I'll see you soon." The sheep smiled and said, "Au revoir" which means 'goodbye, until we meet again' in French. They waved him off and he waved back, then with a last blink of his big white troll eyes he vanished back to his cave in Iceland.

Shortly after the thunder and lightning stopped, the sky brightened at dawn and a beautiful rainbow formed a bridge in the sky; at the end in the distance, a palace appeared and a gate opened up. Then just as they had suddenly appeared, the ghosts vanished into the dawn mists. Some of the Spectral Army, including Captain Archibald Cunningham who relinquished his command to Septimius Severus Constantius, made their way over the rainbow bridge to vanish forever to a new world.

Old Wink-a-Puss prepared himself for bed. It was a little chilly, so he popped his stripy blue and white night shirt on and his matching night cap with a fancy soft bobble on the end. "Goodnight all and thank you." And with that, he retired for the day.

The next evening, Hekla and Freya sent a "Thank you" letter to the Lilts troll on behalf of the flock and themselves via Barry the bat, and Mr Wink-a-Puss continued his night watch.

Farmer Joe, Beryl, Jenny, Bouncer and the flock couldn't make it all out. Everything was as it had been, there were no missing sheep and the flocks on the hills looked fine, the barn roof was back intact. Beryl made everyone a nice hot chocolate drink and gave them a homemade flapjack. That night they all slept like logs.

On the lawn of Poshington Hall on her way to work, Hazel the admissions clerk found a small piece of seaweed paper with gold lettering on it. She couldn't make head nor tail of the inscription, but thought it unusual, so kept it as a bookmark.